Ruby
and the
NOISY HIPPO

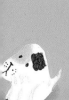

To Sarah and
Laurel and Hardy
under the bed

KINGFISHER
An imprint of Kingfisher Publications Plc
New Penderel House, 283-288 High Holborn, London WC1V 7HZ

First published in hardback by Kingfisher 2000
First published in paperback by Kingfisher 2001
2 4 6 8 10 9 7 5 3 1
1TR/0301/TWP/SG/170ARM

Text and illustrations copyright © Helen Stephens 2000

A CIP catalogue record for this book is available from the British Library.

ISBN 0 7534 0623 3

Printed in Singapore

Ruby and the NOISY HIPPO

Helen Stephens

KINGFISHER

La!

La! La!

Bang!

Bang!

Bang!

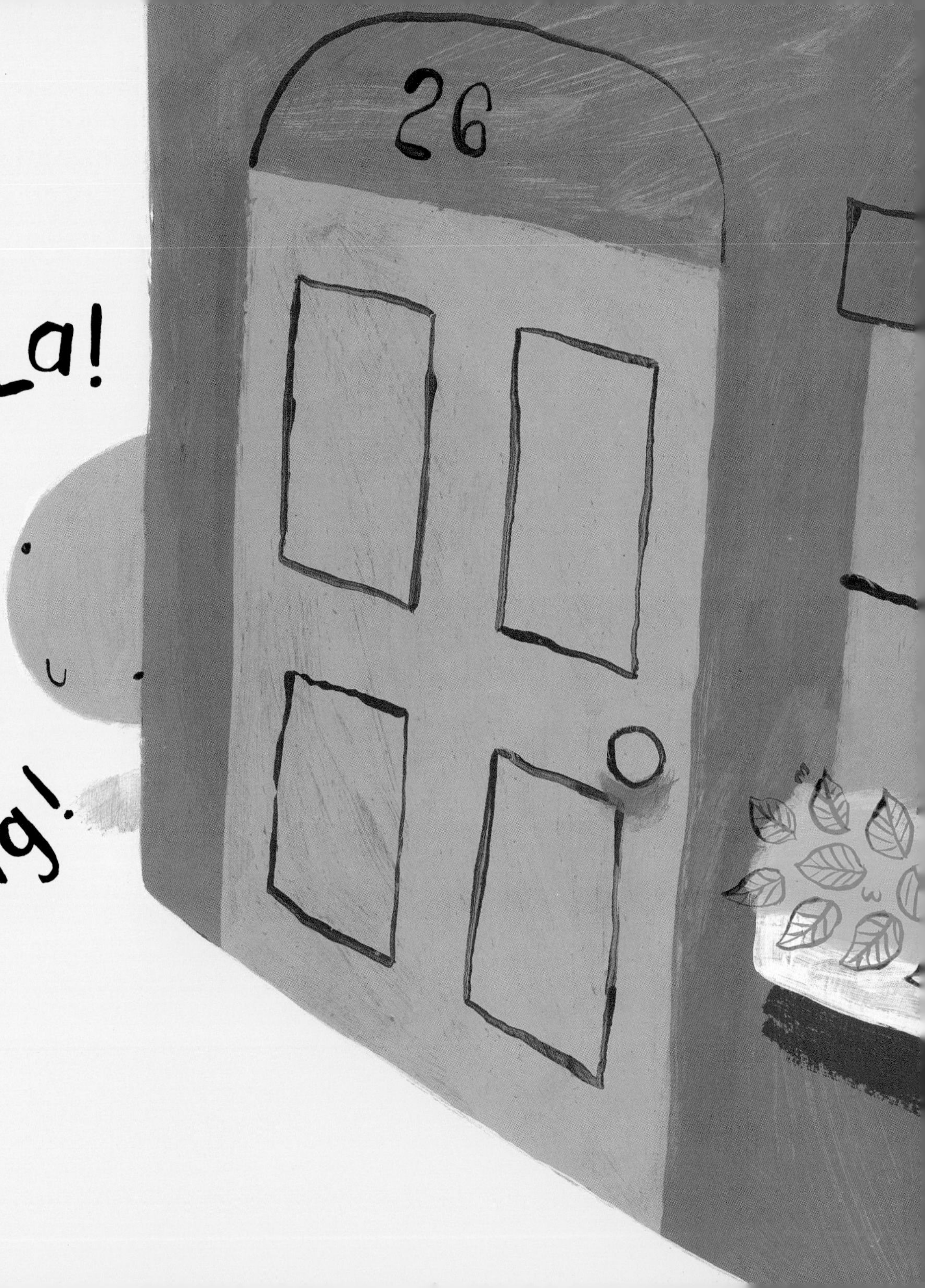

"What is that awful noise?" said Ruby.

"IT'S ME!" shouted Hippo.

"Can I come to the sweet shop with you?"

"Well . . . only if you promise
to be very quiet," said Ruby,
"or people will stare!"

"I promise," whispered Hippo.

And he was very quiet. For a little while . . .

But by the time they reached the postbox, Hippo was singing.
"Be quiet!" said Ruby. "You promised!"

By the time they reached the telephone box, Hippo was singing at the top of his voice.

La!
La!
La!
La!

By the time they reached the bus stop,
Hippo was singing and stamping his feet.

"That's it!" said Ruby. "You're too noisy. People are staring. You can't come to the sweet shop with me!"

Bang!
Bang!
Bang!

"Poor me," whispered Hippo.

Then he had an idea.

Hippo followed Ruby secretly . . .

all the way to the sweet shop.

"One bag of strawberry fizz bombs, please," said Ruby.

closed

space ships

Then she went outside with her sweets.

Suddenly, a great big sweet-eating
monster jumped out at Ruby.
"Give me your strawberry fizz bombs!"
he shouted.

Ruby was scared. Too scared to move.
Too scared to make a sound.

Bang! Bang!

Hippo stomped out of the bushes.
"LEAVE MY FRIEND ALONE!"

The monster ran home crying.

"Thank you, Hippo," said Ruby.
"Maybe it's OK to be noisy sometimes."

Then Ruby and Hippo walked home
together, singing and stamping their feet.